A Cup of Tea
Refresh the Mind

Editing & Compiling
S Afrose

Ukiyoto Publishing

All global publishing rights are held by

Ukiyoto Publishing

Published in 2024

Contents Copyright ©® to the authorized writers

ISBN 9789367956229

All rights reserved.

No part of this publication may be reproduced, transmitted, or stored in a retrieval system, in any form by any means, electronic, mechanical, photocopying, recording or otherwise, without the prior permission of the publisher.

The moral rights of the author have been asserted.

This is a work of fiction. Names, characters, businesses, places, events, locales, and incidents are either the products of the author's imagination or used in a fictitious manner. Any resemblance to actual persons, living or dead, or actual events is purely coincidental.

This book is sold subject to the condition that it shall not by way of trade or otherwise, be lent, resold, hired out or otherwise circulated, without the publisher's prior consent, in any form of binding or cover other than that in which it is published.

www.ukiyoto.com

DEDICATION

To all the dearest Parents
of the authors
of this book.

ACKNOWLEDGEMENT

Thanks a lot Dear Almighty for blessing me always.

Thank you so much dear parents, friends, readers, well-wishers.

You, all are the supporters for making the cutest ever, my dear poetry world.

Special thanks ... To Ukiyoto Publishing Platform for helping this book in the real form. Thanks dear Editorial Board.

Thank you so much dear authors, for your writes to make this canvas such a poetic one. May this ride move on as usual, without any restriction for spreading the hidden gem of peace all over the universe.

Love for all, from the deepest core of my heart.

Poetic love as a cup of tea or coffee…

From Author Desk

© S Afrose

Dhaka, Bangladesh, *(23rd Oct'24)*.

Contents

Fragrance of Tea   1
Open Invitation   5
At a glance: 7

Poems of author Brenda Mohammed   *9*
A cup of tea   12
A cup of coffee   13
A cup of cappuccinoa   14
Refreshment   15
A breakfast drink   16

Poems of author Dr. Sudha Dixit   *17*
Haiku 1   19
Haiku 2   20
A cup of tea   21
Haiku 3   22
Haiku 4   23

Poems of author Angela Kosta   *24*
Careless girl   26
Waiting for love   27

Poems of author Kathy Jo Bryant   *28*
He spilled his tea   30
Tea of herbs   31
A delightful refreshment   32

A kettle of tea	33
A cup to share	34

Poems of author Bogdana Gageanu — *35*

Tea	37
Coffee	38
Wonderland	39

Poems of author Eva Petropoulou Lianou — *40*

Tea	43
It's a cup of tea	44
Coffee or tea	45

Poem of author Kieu Bich Hau — *46*

Two books	48

Poems of author Alexander Kabishev — *49*

Big Tree	52
Gandhi	53
Silence	54
Space	55
Faith	56

Poems of author Dr. Kang Byeong-Cheol — *57*

The sway of bamboo forest	60
The song of sunshine	61
Self-portrait	62
Old alley	63

The teaching of clouds	64

Poems of author Kujtim Hajdari — *65*
Come, join with us.	67
Under shadows of palm	68
Don't disturb kids' smiles	69
Summer smiles to us	70
The kid-hood turn again	71

Poem of author Nageh Ahmed — *72*
My poetry is mixed with coffee	74

Poem of author Vasanth Kumar VP — *75*
Relaxation	77

Poem of author Lungi Shigo Msusa — *79*
A cup of tea	81

Poems of author S Afrose — *83*
The morning calls	85
A cup of tea	86
A cup of coffee	87
Tea or Coffee	88
Black Coffee	89
Be happy	90
One evening	91
Bring me back	93
Exhausted	94

Same tune	95
Just shut up	97
A moment	98
With my friend	99
Today can't forget	100
Just a sip	101
Cool	102
Midst the night	103
Any Coffee?	104
The boiling water	105
Mood off	107
Show off	109
They are	111
Evening Tea Party	114
Bring your joy	115
Hope this time	116
A sweet moment	117
Once a time	119
The time of my life	120
Soothing breeze	121
Ready	122
One drop more	123
Due to Rain	124
The garden is open	125
My day of sight	126
Pebbles	127
The Banayan Tree	128

SURPRISE	*130*
Willy!Willy!	132
Hues!	135
Paint your Pain!	140
Only for you!	141
About the Author	*143*

Fragrance of Tea

Oh my dear!
What's up?
Losing your mind, for a while???
Hold on.
Join with me
Here on the table
A cup of tea...
What a fragrance!
Your mind will be refreshed.
Don't lose this time.
Just come and share
Your hidden tears
With each sip of that tea...
And then...
Refresh the Mind!

Vibes of life,,, Getting the turning point as usual
Now come and dance
With this fragrance of mind-
Thoughts of beautiful minds.
Would you like to be here?
To be my peer
To refresh the mind, so rare...

Editing & Compiling by S Afrose

"A cup of tea"

"It's a poetry book, collection of writes of various writers, around the world.

Each one is the true lover of this realm, a true friend for a cup of tea or coffee"

They try to show the way of how can refresh the mind? How can be relaxed? How can off the exhausted rite? What's the meaning of a cup of tea or coffee? And so on...

Make your time.

May be you can see the hidden gem here, with the glamour of words.

On behalf of the authors, I approach my apology, for any kind of mistake or unwanted word.

Thanks!

Copyright ©S Afrose, Dhaka, Bangladesh, (23rd Oct'24).

2nd time, working as a part of the editorial team

(My apology for any kind of misperception)

Let's enjoy this book: A Cup of Tea

Editing & Compiling by S Afrose

Open Invitation

Hello!Hello!

Would you like to be my friend?

Would you like to take a cup of tea or coffee?

Your mind is seeking someone. Your friend dear. Here, on the table a cup of tea.

Come on.

No objection.

 Each sip asks you one thing. Are you enjoying? Are you overcoming? What?

The time that heals your mind. Refreshing…

So many ones, with various flavors of tea. Just wow!

At a glance, the soothing chamber midst the universe. So?

Would you not like to enjoy some exceptional poems???

Don't be late. Just come on and enjoy this lane. You will be amazed anyway, my dear friend.

Thanks!

© S Afrose,BD. **23rd Oct'24.**

6 Editing & Compiling by S Afrose

At a glance:

Editing & Compiling by S Afrose

Poems of author Brenda Mohammed
Trinidad and Tobago

Brenda Mohammed from Trinidad and Tobago, is a former Bank Manager; who published 61 books in multiple genres and wrote a five-series screenplay for her sci-fi thriller Zeeka Chronicles: Revenge of Zeeka. Among her publications are 18 poetry books of enlightening poems.

Brenda's genres include memoirs, science fiction, romance, self-help, mystery thrillers, children's books, psychological thrillers, christian books, poetry, and poetry anthologies.

She has conducted book signings, hosted Book Fairs in Trinidad and Tobago, and donated books to schools, libraries, and churches.

She is an advocate for Peace, Suicide Prevention, and Against Domestic Violence.

Brenda is the Founder of the Facebook Forum, 'How to Write for Success Literary Network,' and National President for Trinidad and

Tobago of the International Chamber of Writers and Artists [CIESART] – Spain

A cup of tea

In our culture tea has a sentimental value.
Offering a cup of tea to someone symbolizes hospitality.
For the Japanese, it is not simply a physical act when they drink tea.
It's a way to engage with the world around them, in harmony.

Sharing tea has a spiritual meaning of sav ouring the moment.
It's enjoying the inner peace, and bonding with a guest.
There's a possibility you may not have that opportunity again.
So we sit and chat with a cup of tea and pastries.

In China, tea drinking reflects harmony, respect, purity, and tranquillity.
The art of brewing and serving tea is a meditative practice.
Internationally, to mark special occasions there are tea ceremonies.
Tea is served at weddings, births, funerals, and garden parties.

A cup of coffee

One of the most popular drinks in the world is coffee.

Consumers drink around 400 billion cups yearly.

Low doses of caffeine may cause increased alertness.

Higher doses may have negative effects such as anxiety and restlessness.

The cumulative research reflects a health benefit.

Caffeine acts as a central nervous system stimulant.

While it makes you more alert and focused,

Coffee can also irritate and make you anxious.

Caffeine can cause insomnia, and increased heart rate,

Larger doses might cause headaches and chest pain.

There are 25 million small producers who earn a living on coffee.

Coffee is the most popular drink internationally.

A cup of cappuccinoa

I feel refreshed when I drink a Cappuccino on a morning.
It's an espresso-based coffee drink with a special flavouring.
It has an enticing aroma and a layer of milk foam.
When I drink it I never want to leave my home.

Cappuccino has antioxidant properties that help memory loss.
Coffee or tea without sugar or milk assists in weight loss.
A cappuccino with non-fat milk is a low-calorie option.
For a weight loss diet, it is a suitable addition.

Cappuccino lowers the risk of cardiovascular ailments.
It is also useful in preventing skin problems.
If you have not tried it yet, try cappuccino with breakfast today.
It is good for your health and will keep you alert all day.

Refreshment

Whether it is Tea, Coffee, or Cappuccino,
People will always want to feel refreshed.
They are willing to take their chances,
On whatever drink suits their preferences.

Each drink has good points and bad points.
Some people love to wake up and smell the coffee.
Others prefer to drink cappuccino and stay healthy.
Yet some love to start their day with a cup of tea.

Everyone has choices to make and it's up to them.
Choose your drinks with care and stay healthy.
Life is short and we must do what we can to survive.
Before we take that first sip say cheers to life.

A breakfast drink

It's a family fun ritual every sunrise,
As you awaken to the chirping of the birds outside.
The swaying of the branches in the breeze,
That miserable alarm clock does not please.

You run downstairs to the kitchen sink,
For water to brew your favourite morning drink.
The addictive smell opens your eyes to a new day.
A brimming cup makes you happy and gay.

Without it, you cannot survive the day's tasks,
Luckily we are no longer required to wear masks.
Each sip adds spunk to everything you do.
People all over the world love a breakfast drink too.

Poems of author Dr. Sudha Dixit

India

Sudha Dixit was born and brought up in UP and she is presently settled in Bangalore. She is doing what she always wanted to do - painting landscapes and portraits & writing poetry/articles on the net and in various magazines, including print media.

She looks at nature with myopic eyes & paints it wearing tinted glasses, with poetry in her heart. Poetry just happens. It acts as catharsis in her life, removing the toxin from her heart in the form of words on paper. It's therapeutic. This high-spiritedness reveals itself in both, her poems & paintings.

Haiku 1

I'm relaxing with
A cup of steaming hot tea
In a state of bliss.

Haiku 2

What's your preference
Hot tea, cold coffee, or me?
Better decide fast.

A cup of tea

The steam rising from
The cup of hot tea
Transports me to a
Fairyland, so pretty.

Transforms me into
A philosopher
With tantalizing
Dreams to offer.

Dreams put me on road
To walk searching goal
Tea is the real
Instigating tool.

Face the challenges
In life with aplomb,
Hold a cup of tea
In hand to keep calm .

Haiku 3

Aroma of that
Coffee brewing's hypnotic
Reminds me of you.

Haiku 4

Just so much I wish
Coffee, you, I, and some rain
And life, paradise.

24 Editing & Compiling by S Afrose

Poems of author Angela Kosta

Albania

Angela Kosta was born in Albania in and has lived in Italy since 1995. Executive Director of the magazine MIRIADE, translator, essayist, journalist, literary critic and promoter. She has published 15 books: novels, poems and fairy tales in Albanian, Italian, Turkey and English. Her publications have appeared in various literary magazines and newspapers in various states. Angela Kosta translates and writes articles and interviews for the newspaper "Calabria Live", Saturno magazine, the newspaper "Le Radici", the international magazine "Orfeu", Alessandria Today magazine, the Nacional newspaper, the Gazeta Destinacioni, the magazine Perqasje Italo - Shqiptare , the international magazine Atunis - Belgium, collaborates with magazines in Lebanon, International Literature Language Journal (USA), Turkey, Morocco, Bangladesh, Iraq, etc.

Careless girl

On this special day

Soft snow settles on my eyelids.

I collect fifty white roses

Beautiful fresh as the years of my life...

I would like to go back in time

When little girl running

I was happy

When technology didn't chain my body

Now a prisoner of TV, computer, cell phone.

I wish I was the carefree girl again,

Knowing how happy it would make me.

Today on this spring day

I feel at peace with everything around me.

I savor and sip this cup of coffee,

With taste laughing

I love this day...

I love the sun...

I admire the beautiful and fresh roses

Like the years of my life.

Waiting for love

I've been waiting
for you
past midnight
with a hot cup of tea,
watching the pouring rain on the cold, dark glass.
Beyond the heated and fogged halo
from my interminable wait for love...

Poems of author Kathy Jo Bryant

USA

A Cup of Tea

Kathy Jo Bryant hails from Missouri, USA.

She is a genealogist, the author of a published two volume genealogy, and the member of two lineage societies. She has received many accolades for her poetry. She is the author of four poetry books on Amazon and lulu: Golden Glowing Mushroom, Favorite Things in My World, Matchless Mosaic, and Maw Maw's Begonias.

Her work is in quite a few poetry groups and themed anthologies, such as Sweetycat Press, McKinley Publishing Hub, and for other authors. She is a member of, and former moderator for, the growing Facebook poetry group: "The Passion of Poetry."

He spilled his tea

When I was young and growing up,
We gathered Sasafrass root, for tea in a cup.

We loved the taste, and sipped with joy,
We cousins did, this tea, enjoy.

So cousin, George, was drinking his tea,
But it suddenly spilled, embarrassed was he.

For it soaked his crotch, & his face turned red,
He ran like the wind, to his house, instead.

I never forgot this, at Gram's & Gramp's,
Some might have laughed & gotten cramps!

Tea of herbs

Tea is refreshing
and soothes right down to your toes
Herbal teas give health.

A delightful refreshment

Many are the delightful teas,
To refresh, from around the world,

A reason for friendly gatherings,
A pat on the back, arms around us, curled.

A kettle of tea

A whistling kettle, puffs out steam,
With a cheerful, comforting sound,
The water will then be nice and hot,
For the tea, eagerly passed around.

A cup to share

Caring is sharing,

A pot of tea,

A cup for some friends,

And a cup for me.

Poems of author Bogdana Gageanu

Romania

Bogdana Găgeanu is a poetess and a playwright . She has been published in anthologies and magazines. Her playwrights have been heard to different radios.She received a lot of international awards.

She was interviewed by Loi Monroe,Gelda Castro,Helen Sarita, Dustin Pickering, Dennis Brown, Eva Lianou Petropoulou.

She likes to inspire.

She wrote two books of poems,"My soul pyramid " in English and " The soul from the ink pot" in Romanian.

She wrote a script for a short Romanian movie called "GPS" , presented at a film festival in France.

She won a " MENZIONE" Award at Amilcare Solferini Contest.

Tea

Tea in a beautiful afternoon
With a relaxing flavour
That remind us of meditation
Of being quiet and never rushing.
Just a sip of tea
Then , another sip
Stopping the seconds of time
In just one drink .

Coffee

Coffee is so good
Coffee is the refreshing drink
That you need to wake up.
A good coffee is a good energizer
In order to have a good day.
A cup is more attractive
When it is filled with an attractive drink.
Coffee is the magic potion.

Wonderland

We are in Wonderland
Where a sip of liquid
Can make you bigger or smaller.
Where Mr.Rabbit always is in a hurry
And Mr. Hatter is always coming,
To drink his cup of tea
At the exact time.
The Wonderland of liquid.

Poems of author Eva Petropoulou Lianou

Greece

Eva Petropoulou Lianou is an Internationally awarded author. She has published many books and eBooks. Her work has been included in the Greek Encyclopedia Haris Patsis, p. 300. Her books have been approved by the Ministry of Education and Culture of Cyprus, for the Student and Teacher library.

Presidente of European continent,

Juventudes Academy Mundial Argentina.

Presidente of Greece association,

Mille Minds of Mexico.

Official candidate Nobel Peace prize

President
Representative of Global UHE Peru
Greece.

Editor in chief
Acheron Magazine
Vietnam
Greece.

World Ambassador of
Academy of Ethics India.

Tea

We drink it as a hope every afternoon
For some it is a culture,
For others it's a special tradition;
For others it's a memory of
Beautiful life.

It's a cup of tea

War cannot stop the life.
We drink a cup of tea
Laugh is coming to our face,
Perfume of our orange tree is coming in our sense.
A cup of tea with friends
Can bring back,
Our peace in mind.

Coffee or tea

They exist people of coffee,

People of tea.

It is a matter of belief.

A matter of character

Who is drinking tea,

Will not accept the coffee time,

That coffee machine that tradition away.

Life is like a tea leave who is just talking strength from sun ray in the fields.

Poem of author Kieu Bich Hau

Vietnam

A Cup of Tea

Kieu Bich Hau is a poet, editor. Acts as Media Director of SaVipharm and Founder and Head of Hanoi Female Translators

Her writes have achieved 9 awards till now on this literature field. Like as-

The ART Danubius Prize in 2022 for her nurturing and deepening Vietnamese-Hungarian literary and cultural relations.

The Great Award of Korea 2023 for her devotement in promotion Vietnamese poetry and prose on an international level.

Published 25 books of prose, poetry, essay in Vietnam, Italy, Canada.

Her poems and short stories have been translated into many foreign lan**guages (17)**: English, Italian, Korean, Russian, Marathi, Hindi, Romanian, Hungarian, Spanish, Portuguese, Nepali, Uzbek, French, German, Turkish, Chinese, Montenegrin.

Email: kieubichhau@gmail.com

Two books

You write a book of the future,

The book of thoughts

It brings about sufferings.

I write a book of what's happening,

The book of the present

It brings about happiness.

We are lovers of life.

Life is a masterpiece.

Live it by our hearts,

Create it by our souls.

All of us

Master of our minds.

Poems of author Alexander Kabishev

Russia

Kabishev Alexander Konstantinovich - President of the Youth Union of Writers (YUW). Academician of MARLEY. Poet and writer, founder of a new trend in literature and art - choism. Volunteer journalist of the magazine "POET", active participant and director of the magazine at the foundation "LIFE LINE OF EVERY CHILD", founder and director of the international creative and cultural project "DEMO GOG", editor-in-chief of the magazine "HUMANITY", author of the collection of stories "NIGHTMARE", collection of poems "DANCE OF POETRY", novel "RED CORAL". Curator and organizer of collections of modern prose and poetry "SILICON AGE" (2 volumes), collection "WHISPERS IN THE WIND", the first Russian-Vietnamese collection "DAWN", the first Russian-Serbian collection "FRIENDSHIP". Director of the documentary film about charity "ECLF". Founder and mentor of the world record project - HYPERPOEM. Member of the Russian Union of Writers. Member of the Union of Writers of North America. Co-author of many collections and publications in magazines and online media. A number of his original works have been translated and published in Spanish, Arabic, Italian, Vietnamese, French, English, Hindi, Portuguese, Serbian, Greek, Tagalog and other languages (Russia, St. Petersburg).

Big Tree

You see in forest tall green tree
Which separates in top to three-
What three? You ask, my answer is-
Believe, the honest and mind peace.

It's difficult imagine so,
Someone could say - You thinking slow!
But I am dreamer - this my part,
I can't see reason to give up.

I hope, believe and even know,
I can find friends who thinking so,
No need to change some in myself
They will accept me too as well.

And then, if I the forest tree,
Someway they also can same be.
Together forest we which grow
And our dreams just special know.

Gandhi

One famous person in the past,
Whose plan so wise as century lasts,
Was like a point for kind and love
And heart for people all enough.

He changed the time, he changed mankind.
And even enemies had opined,
That he was greatest top in mind
As well as answers reach and find.

He was like father for us all,
We follow his advice by soul,
The people changed but life his not,
That's something never we forgot!

Silence

Sometimes you want talk
And make your mind walk,
But also there are some days
When silence is like way.

Is that so bad,
Makes you feel mad?
Will you agree,
And this also see?

Silence is hell
You can't get or tell,
Other what mean
As well what you feel.

Space

Space outside and its inside
The mean of world space really wide,
We can find space around us
When even traveling in bus.

But what is space?
Let's test discuss
I guess this is interesting
So we will no pass.

We live in space
Or space in us?
We study since of space
Or it's of us?

We are material
As world and planet, stars… Forgot!
But space is not material
And full, but this is also really cool.

Why? My answer - Not
Material will never stop
And we all people, pets or plant
Need space to be as creature done!

Faith

What is my faith?
And what is faith for you?
I will answer soulmate,
Why winter of the hope still so blew!

For us all faith has many ways,
We choose it, find or follow, miss,
Look to the person close to you
This can be answer to all this.

What is all faith?
What are we all?
Faith always answer-
As I know…

Poems of author Dr. Kang Byeong-Cheol

Korea

Dr. Kang Byeong-Cheol is a Korean author, poet, translator, and holder of a Doctor of Philosophy in Political Science degree. He was born in Jeju City, South Korea in 1964, and began his writing career in 1993. His first short story, "Song of Shuba," was published when he was twenty-nine years old.

In 2005, Dr. Kang published a collection of short stories and has since won four literature awards, publishing over eight books in total. He was a member of The Writers in Prison Committee (WiPC) of PEN International from 2009 to 2014. From 2018 to 2022, he served as Secretary General of the Jeju Unification Education Center. Prior to that, he was a Specially Appointed Professor at Jeju International University from 2016 to 2018, a Research Professor at Chungnam National University National Defense Institute from 2013 to 2016, a Senior Researcher at the Society of Ieodo Research from 2010 to

2017, and CEO of Online News Media Jejuin News from 2010 to 2013.

Dr. Kang also works as an editorial writer for Jeminilbo, a newspaper in Jeju City, Korea. Currently, he holds the position of Vice President at The Korean Institute for Peace and Cooperation.

The sway of bamboo forest

The green forest sways with grace,
Telling me the wind's in place.

I sit and sip, at perfect ease,
Enjoying coffee with the breeze.

The song of sunshine

Without light, no shadow,
Bright and true,
Light never lose little crack, it shines right through.
Don't give up, though times are tough,
To live means embracing the smooth and the rough.
Even dark clouds have a light side.

Self-portrait

Like anyone else, I found my way,
Married, had kids, and watched them play.
And as I aged, with time I blend,
Becoming stardust in the end.

Old alley

No footprints left, just dust in air,
The wind and cat both wander there.
A life has passed, now leaves descend,
I rest where history does not end.

The teaching of clouds

I lift my eyes to skies so wide,
Where grass and trees in seasons glide,
Mountains and rivers shift their hue,
Dancing in life's rhythm, ever true.

Fragile creatures, too weak to stay,
In winter's cold, they fade away.
Yet with the morning's rising light,
The mountains' heart beats with new might.

The clouds drift softly, far and high,
Their shapes transform as they pass by.
A silent sound they leave behind:
The world is ever-changing, we find.

In stillness, wisdom may be found-
Nothing lasts forever, round and round.

Poems of author Kujtim Hajdari

Albania

Kujtim Hajdari is an Albanian poet and translator, was born in Albania. He graduated from the university for Albanian language and literature and worked for many years as a high school teacher in Albania. Recently, lives in the USA.

He has written many volumes of poetry in Albanian, Italian and recently in English. He won many national and international competitions and received many recognitions. In August 2024, he was the winner of the International Impact Book Awards in the USA.

He has participated so far in 72 national and international magazines and anthologies.

His poetry has been publishing in more than 20 countries in the world.

Come, join with us.
(Haiku)

Summer smiles us,
The beach - hugs all the people,
The waves applaud.

Don't know how happy,
When merge myself in the songs,
Of crowds sings around.

The skins like chocolate,
The sun paints them so sweetly,
As a master painter does.

Come, join with us,
The summer flow, goes speedy,
It's far its return.

Under shadows of palm
(Tanka)

Was a dream this day,
to read my favorite books,
in relax's magic.
The summer brought me this gift,
and the palm kisses sweetly.

Was the dream this day
Under the shadows of palm
siping cold coffee
In peaceful and relaxing
Forgetting the running world.

Don't disturb kids' smiles
(Senryu)

He is in his relax,
Makes and unmakes the castles,
Raising the sand castles
Shouting the waves

Then wets the beachgoers,
And smiles them highly voice,
Who takes from his joy.

He discovers the world,
Can you make him happier?
Give him a big smile!

The world needs enough,
The future calls us today:
Don't disturb kids' smiles!

Summer smiles to us
(A day of summer)

This summer's day arrived with a smile,
With fragrance of beautiful morning,
With sunshine and flowers in hands,
And I touch and get drunk in its delight.

And if I am sad and weary,
The clouds of my thoughts bring me rain,
I can't let it not to take me,
In its arm full of sweetness.

I was born for the sweet summer,
And it has come just for me,
Would I have convinced it,
If I said, "I don't love it."

We sat embraced until late,
The mist fell on fields and forests,
Each of us dreams and loves,
In the sleep covered with stars.

Around us, the world spins heavily,
And it, may be, can't see the summer's beauty,
But the summer makes place for all the world,
It caresses and gives a hug to everybody.

The kid-hood turn again

In this beautiful relaxing days,
Enjoying the sea and sun-rays,
The kid-hood returns our memories,
And makes us laugh with our stories.

Each of us has remained in soul,
A little kid that returns us whole,
That makes us to game in sand,
Dancing with kids hand by hand.

Poem of author Nageh Ahmed

Egypt

A Cup of Tea

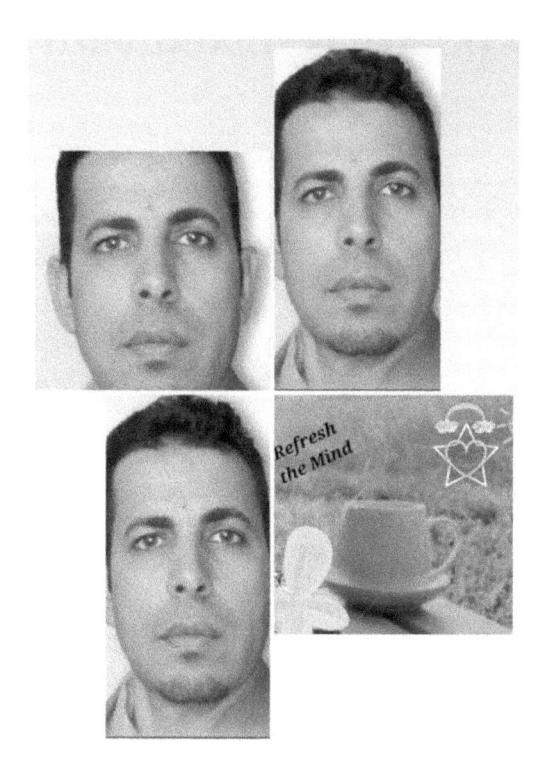

Nageh Ahmed, Egypt, poet, journalist, and international peace ambassador, worked in journalism, and has achieved 2 master's degrees and 8 honorary doctorates.

Birth and address: 1972 AD, Al-Maseed, Al Idwa, Minya, Egypt

Education: Bachelor of Science in Dar Al Uloom 1997, and General Diploma in Education 2013.

Founder of the Poet Nageh Ahmed Club in 2012, and a member, supervisor, and official in many cultural groups.

He has many poems published in print and electronically on local, Arab and international websites, newspapers and magazines.

My poetry is mixed with coffee

My heart beats, craving her kiss.

Her sweet beauty and delicacy inspired me.

Inspiration of the gardens of love and ecstasy

She made me forget wandering and sleep.

How sweet is the taste of her coffee!

Overflow, O' mistress of poetry!

Increase my love and embrace

From the pulse of her fragrant flavor,

More of my poetry will be strong.

A Cup of Tea 75
Poem of author Vasanth Kumar VP
India

Vasanth Kumar VP, professionally a High School Teacher. He is a potential and multi awarded writer . He has written more than 500 poems so far in English. His writes have been publishing in many magazines and anthologies. Received Honorary Doctorate from Nigeria, Global Peacemaker Doctorate from UAE etc.

Interviewed two times by International Literary Forums (USA).

Appointed as Vice -President of Asia and an International Co-ordinator by GLT.

Appointed as a Child Rescue Ambassador by Iqra Foundation.

Appointed as Global Vice President by Nigeria.

International Ambassador, appointed by Morocco.

Humanity Ambassador, appointed by UAE.

An Advisor from Kaduna Nigeria.

Relaxation

Poetry is not just
about eloquent verses
but, it is a powerful tool
for relaxation
and self-care.

Poetry invites us to slow down
reflect, and find moments of peace
and stillness in our busy lives.
Let's make time for relaxation
to be free and calm.

We do not underestimate
relaxation is an art
so, let's embrace it with open arms
it is through rest that we can truly appreciate the beauty of life.

Relaxation is not a luxury
but, a necessity
as it allows us to recharge,
refocus and be more productive
in the long run.

Let poetry guide us
towards relaxation

and help us to find

moments of peace

amidst all the chaos of life.

Poem of author Lungi Shigo Msusa

South Africa

Lungi Christian Msusa but writing as Lungi Shigo Msusa

Born in Eastern Cape Province, South Africa in a town called East London. Moved to Mdantsana township just outside East London when he was still very young to start his first primary school at Sophakama Primary school. His parents are from Tsolo a rural village few kilometers away from Mthatha so his roots are from Tsolo. His origins are from Tsolo.

His love for writing started after he stopped working in 2019 to pursue his dream of writing poetry and small stories.

His love for poetry came as the product of his love for reading literature, any kind of Literature, from novels to autobiographies and poetry.

A cup of tea

A cup of tea
A cup of love
From her window
To mine it surfaces
In love's aroma.

A smell so above
A brew so loving
My heart so longing
An invitation so overwhelming.

I knock on the aroma
Love opens, hearts skip a bit.
The aroma so overwhelming
I kiss the aroma with a loving heart ,
Introducing me as a bachelor upstairs.

All whys answered lovingly
Love tea readily brewing.
A cup of tea, a cup of love
Thanks God she's my cup of tea.

Over a cup of tea new love born
Under the aroma love kiss,

On my way out I ask her name-
"Come back for the nightcap
 You'll know everything about me".

A cup of tea, my cup of tea.
The difference was the same
A tea brewed, love joined.
Two hearts became one
Best tea drank my heart.

Poems of author S Afrose

Bangladesh

Author S Afrose has made her realm since August-2020. Her writes have been publishing on magazines and anthologies (90+). In this writing realm, she has achieved many awards (beyond her expectations)

Published author of 31 poetry books- available on amazon worldwide and other sites.

Educational achievements- B Pharm, M Pharm (JU,BD.)

Contact-sabihapoetryparadise24@gmail.com, sabiha_pharma@yahoo.com, afrosewritings@outloook.cm

YouTube: S Afrose *Muse of Writes*(@safrose_poetic_arts)

Facebook Page: Muse of Words by S Afrose

Twitter:@afrose2020

Inst. @safrosepoetryworld

The morning calls

Working
All the time

With
Dearest mind

A connection.

A call

Omnipotent for all

Though not now

Still can feel

The morning calls.

A cup of tea

Yes I agree
This time
Only you and I
And the serenity,
A cup of tea.

May be
You are right
Simply the best
Your mind
Free from exhausted rite.

A cup of coffee

Look at the table

Two cups

Waiting

For what

My favourite hut.

A cup of Coffee

Let's enjoy

This morning

With a new opening

What do you think?

Tea or Coffee

What do you like
To take

Tea or Coffee?

You can't understand
Once again
I repeat.

Just a beverage
With this beautiful environment
Then go ahead.

Black coffee

Chill dear!
Of course you will get
Your favourite layer
With each sip,
A cup of Coffee.

Black Coffee!
I see.
Now hold the cup
And relax,
Forgetting that unwanted pool.

Be happy

Not so easy
Not so tough
Still can say,
Be happy
My sweet heart.

Be happy
When you hold
That cup of tea,
As my friend
At last.

Sooner or later
You will feel better,
Just accept this part.
On the stage- the art
Your hidden grudges.

One evening

A memorable time
One evening
When I was on the road
Of that garden
Could hear some words,
What's in your mind?

Though nothing
But till the night
I could feel
Something very strange
From that evening.

Brain can't sleep
Mind can't feel
I see
Something is here
With a good flavour.

A mug
Full of creamy layer,
With a spoon
And a bag of tea
Or coffee, soon.

One evening

Turns into
A melody
Of the life,
I agree this time.

Bring me back

No
I will not stop
So?
Bring me back
My song.

Lost song!
My lost song!

So long
I completely understand
I completely agree.
Still I can't believe
Lost song like your favourite tune.

That song
Makes me happy,
When I am sad
Off mood always,
I can get the dearest palace.

That palace
Full of fragrance
Of the Coffee,
The aroma
So chilled.

Exhausted

What can I say?
What can you see?
What's that ray???

Experience so bad
Exhausted mind sets
Who is saying that???

I want to play
With a free mind
No more Exhausted signs.

How can beat?
Let's think it.
Would you like...
A Cup of Tea or Coffee???

Wow!
That's so nice
I like that
Definitely I will be...

Same tune

Say safe
Stay safe
Same tune
For each step.

Fireworks
Fireballs
From your mind
Now hold the knob.

You can't escape
You want to stop
Just relax.

Take your time
You can hear
The same tune.

Go there
Your dearest peer
The Coffee table.

Hold the mug
Set the goal
Then clarify.

Closed eyes
You smile now,
How amazing!

Just shut up

Oh you!
Again!

Killing myself
Just go to hell.

Just shut up.
Hear the words.

Mind blusts
Anger can't hold
Dramatically fallen
The beautiful layer.

Ah!Ah!
Pls stop.
Why?
Just shut up.

A moment

This is so special
Watching the snowfall,
Waiting for you
Without playing any role.

Yep!
A moment!
Very special. for me
Yes dear!

Wait.
That table
Holding the moment,
When you will come
As a serene phase
Will get a cup of tea.

I love you
Can't say,
A moment
Holds my day
As an engraved ray.

With my friend

Need to talk
Need to share
Nobody is near
Then?

Take the point.
Your tea
Your coffee,
What do you like?

Will be your friend
Trust me.

With my friend
I have spent
After a long
A beautiful evening
Can't imagine.

A Cup of Tea
Brings me
My lost sense
My lost smile,
Amazing!

Today can't forget

Today is beautiful
Today is cool.
You said once
Don't dare to forget
My heart.

Today don't forget
My heart is ready
To say you
How valuable your smile
In my life?

See,
Waiting and waiting…
Finally can see
The smiley face of
Dearest parents.

Just a sip

Sitting all alone
The waves from the wind's core
Come to touch and disturb
My little and tiny paradise.

I say You can't stop me here
I say You are too much naughty dear
Pls sit here for a while
Then can feel how much time I can share.

Obviously it's all about love
The reflection of the sweet mind
Reflection of the dearest life
For a while just forget dear.

Would you like to join me
With a cup of tea or coffee?
If you take a sip
You will get the original peace.

As the divine peace is here
Coming and soothing all the tears,
Letting know hello dear
I am here and also you are.

Cool

So cool.
A cup of tea or coffee
Just hold the cup.

All tiredness just have gone
You and I the best peers
Now let me know this time
Let me show this universe.

Finally we can see the canvas
How can I and you share?
Will you take a sip here?
The soothing charm, my dear!

Midst the night

Midst the night I wake up
Mind asks what's up?
What do you want to do
What do you want to like?

I don't understand what can
What is that my dear friend
Who will be here with me
I need the company of my friend.

Hey you!
Don't worry.
I am here
Your dear mind.

You can spend some time
With me for anything dear
Let's celebrate this time
How do you like a soothing charm?

Any coffee?

I think,
That's fine
Can see you, dear.

Finally beneath azure's canvas
The beautiful journey of this life
With the glamour of the mind
With all the glittering stars.

Midst night when wake up
Feeling so bad my dear,
You offer- any coffee?
I love to see and say,,,

You are my genuine love.
Let's take this coffee together.

The boiling water

The gas cooker
Holding the kettle
The boiling water.

Some ingredients of leaves
Tea or coffee
I can't breathe now.

The kettle
Making some noises
A joint venture.

Hey you!
Who?
Why are you here?

You break my dream
Now?
What's up?

Oh sorry!
My dear!
I will be your smile.
Together
We can build

The lovely bridge of this earth.

A fragrance
From the core of the kettle
Now spreading around the world.

What a friend!
What a fragrance!
Can't imagine dear.

Mood off

Here you are
Jolly mind
Suddenly
The strike of dark.

Mood swing
Mood off.

You say
What's that?
I need a break
Need to refresh the mind.

I see
Let's do this
With soothing charm
Now I get the point.

Mood swing
Mood off.

Not welcome
As I have my own choice
My dearest sign.

A mug of tea
Holds me
And energizes the mind ...

Show off

The set of tea cups
On the table
Midst the garden
Just a glimpses
Show off.

What's that meaning?
Need to clean.
Need to see
That big twist.

Marbles on the garden
Colourful sunday
Making my day
Just hold on.

Show off
No fruitful loop
Take a slope
Just show off.

Find out sign
The magic pine
I take the pie

And then,

Show off
For what's scope?
I say you,
And you say not.

Joy of life
Is the prime contact ?
You can't deny
Just show off the rhyme.

Show the time
I have made
My rhyme,
And then it's the cake time.

Right or not
What can I cope?
I don't get
I need an open pause.

Then take your time
Set the rhyme,
Show off
Don't cry.

They are

They are working there
With their minds
So clear
And then take the sign.

They are here
They can share
Why and why
They are here?

They came
From the heaven
Taking a snap
What's going on here?

They are dragonflies
They are glimpse of minds
They are dragonflies
They are great overall.

And then
Ask the guy-
What are you doing
Are you blind?

In front of
A big pool
You may be dropped
And then cope.

What do you want
Coping the sign
They are dragonflies
Witness of your mind.

You can't escape
This time is the best
You beat the fact
They are here.

After a long
The world can see
What's going on?
Afterall... the dragonflies' mall.

We know
You know
What and why
We are here…

I know
You don't see

Now I can fly

I can share my dream.

Evening tea party

Come on

The evening tea party is ongoing.

Come on

The evening time is waiting.

Come on

The evening sky is wondering.

Come on

The evening wind is amazing.

Come on

The evening party is here.

Come on

And join with us.

Bring your joy

One step ahead
One step back
Bring your smile
Bring your joy.

One step hold
One step back
Bringing the happiness
Bring the peace.

Hope this time

Sing the song
See and shine
Hope this time
I am not fine.

Feel and see
And you see
I am here
I am history of rhyme.

I love to say
I love to share
I will be dear
I am fine.

Hope this time
Everything is fine
I say now
Give me some time.

And that's time.

A sweet moment

With all sets
A new state
A sweet moment
My dear friend.

A sweet hope!
A new rope
Binds all,
How is that comment?

A sweet moment
Literally a lane
And then
A beautiful crane.

Be its part
A cute art
The role of plane
A flying crane.

It asks me
Then stops,
New look!
Again the same slope.

Be my friend
Be my trend
A new slope
A sweet moment.

Be or not
I don't think anymore,
I can take
I can cope.

Be its mind
Be its chime,
Obviously not, why?
It's a sweet moment, dear friend.

Once a time

Again other things
Are here
Making this time
A new sign.
Make it fast
So slow
Previous time
Now the sunshine.

I am here
You are there,
You say- Hi!
I say, never mind.

Be my friend
Be my crane.
I say- Hi
I say again- Hello!

The time of my life

Hope
You will make this time,
The time of my life.

Hope
You will not give up
As peace fallen on your mind.

Your heart
Brave
Beating, so fast.

How sweet!
Nice moments
Nice time.

Soothing breeze

That time was not nice
Mind was such a hostage
Into the cave of the salvage
That day was not cool, at last.

Hold the knob hold the role
Your mind Your favourite pool
You know this so much
You are not welcome, oh dear!

I am sure for a while
I lost my sense of life
Oh dear sweet dreams!
Pls don't go away and make the ring.

Hearing the same song
I can see the paradise
In my hut my dreamy earth
Now can get the soothing breeze.

Ready

Is that clear?
Making this layer
Finally can share,
Ready my dear.

I can hear
Where are your dear?
Sitting on this stair
Finally scary tears.

Oh no.
Don't do this
Don't do that
Make it fast so…

You can hit
You can seat
On that chair,
Hello! Teddy bear!

I can feel
There's no seal
Except my cute reel,
Oh dear reel! Ready?

One drop more

The essence

Of that tea

Now spreads,

And speaks

About the essence of the dearest seal.

One drop more…

I can see

My lost fly.

Oh dear friend

Dear butterfly!

Let me fly

With you for this time

At last.

Due to Rain

Your common sense
No more humours
No more sirens

Due to Rain
You and I
Always share
The same fact.

Due to Rain
Nobody can get
Anything else
Instead
Of the dearest pace.

Oh joy!
My dear pace
Place of heart
Please come back,
And hold me tightly
In your arms, finally.

The garden is open

It's a garden
Full of flowers
Full of free minded arts.
The garden is open for all.
The garden is here
The garden calls all-
Pls come here
And make the harmonious goal.

There
A tea table
A coffee table,
A set of cups and a kettle,
The hot water;
And then...

Snacks, ready.
With the brewing coffee
And also
The lemon tea.

The table is decorated
Holding that stage,
As its owner loves-
Let's do it.

My day of sight

Today is my part
My dear art
My day of sight
My dear plight.

Today is so far
Not welcome dear
My dear art
My dear sweet part.

I touch the part
My song is my heart
How can you survive?
Today is my first sight.

When I am here
I want to share
A beat of the nation
I think this time.

Today cannot define
I know, how can shine?
My dear pine
My dearest sunshine.

Pebbles

On the road
You see
And then say,
Pebbles on the road.

On the road
You tell-
The training will be for the wellness,
And the truth is...

Pebbles on the road-
Pebbles on the road.

The Banyan Tree

Mark this word
And keep it fine.
So?
The Banyan Tree is here.

Mark this time
And then
Title of mind-
A joke or jade of rhyme.

The rhythms!
Inside, no song.
The storm-
Inside a place, full of chaoses.

The Banyan Tree
For all
Making the goal,
Hopefully soon.

Be its favourite.
Be the first
And then,
The great hero of mine.

SURPRISE

A Little Gift With These Poems-

Short Stories:

Willy! Willy!

On the gas burner, a kettle. Inside it, some water. Boiling!!!

Willy! Willy!

Who is that?

A little girl comes out, holding a doll. She is Willy. The kettle asks- now, what do you want to take?

Tea or Coffee?

One more thing, it's a magical Tea pot, Kettle.

It can make any type of tea or coffee, as like as you want.

How can it come here?

That's a big story.

One day, Willy played into the garden.

After some times, she went outside of the garden. All alone.

Suddenly, she could hear something very strange. A sound! MAY BE SOMEONE TRY TO BREAK SOMETHING.

Then she tried to look after, got a little bottle. Inside that, a little thing was flying.

Willy took the bottle. The sound stopped. She heard.- 'Are you angel?'

Willy laughed and told-

'I am Willy. I love all. I help all.'

Then she opened the mouth of the bottle.

That little thing was come out, and turned into a little fairy.

A Cup of Tea

"Thanks a lot Willy.

You help me. You save me.

I am here for a long time. A wizard captured me and locked in that bottle.

Now I am free, as your heart is the purest one.

Thanks a lot again."

Now tell me , what do you want ?

Willy: I don't need anything.

Fairy: Anything? That can help you to help others, may be.

Then, Willy thought a few moments.

Fine, my parents have a coffee machine. But that was broken a few days ago. Couldn't make coffee. So, parents felt helpless. You can help this one.

Fairy: Take this kettle. It's a magical Tea pot., will help to brew the best Tea or Coffee.

You take this one. It can talk. But only you can hear, other can't.

Willy takes the pot. The fairy goes away.

From that time, that kettle is with Willy.

Now , Willy asks for something very special coffee. As her grandparents arrived just now.

The kettle full fills with coffee.

Willy holds the kettle.

She has dropped each drop, carefully.

What a sweet fragrance!

Mind sings song without any sense.

Willy takes the tray of coffee and goes to her grandparents.

Grandparents: Wow!

Willy, you did a great job. You have served this coffee, so nice.

We are proud of you.

Willy: Thanks grandparents.

Time has passed. Now Willy is a young lady.

She opens a Tea corner, a coffee table.

There are so many people.

Each day they come only to take

A sip of the coffee or tea.

After, taking this, they forget their pains.

They feel so relaxed.

They really enjoy their lives.

By this way, Willy helps people to reflect themselves, to refresh their minds.

Copyright ©S Afrose, BD.

20th Oct-24

Hues!

Zara is watching from so far.

A train has been coming since the 9 pm.

But still it's not reached. She is waiting and waiting. During this verse, she has already taken 10 cups of tea. No more today.

What's the reason?

Her friend- Sara, coming after a long gap,,, around 10 years lap. She eagerly waits for this time.

Sara!
Hey Sara!

Where are you?

Come here. I am here.

Then, she is running and running...

Zara holds Sara.

They are best friends.

They know each other heartfully since childhood.

Oh dear Zara!

Glad to see you.

What a surprise!

You have grown such a pretty lady.

Nice to know this time.

Look Sara.

This is too much.

I am not like that.

Of course you are not, but for me you are.

Both of them are laughing...

Hahahahaha!!!

Zara: let's go to my new venture.

I am a master of the tea maker.

I have made so many flavours of the tea.

If you drink once, then can't forget dear.

Sara: oh my God!

You are so talented. Bravo!

I really appreciate.

Anyway, let's go there as soon as.

Morning Dews

This is my tea shop. I have spent most of the time here. Sit.

Oh dear!

Don't say me anything.

I will manage by myself.

Sara takes a chair and then she tries- a cup of tea.

Hey Zara!

Give me a lemon tea.

Okay madam.

Then she smiles loudly hahahahaha!

A sip reminds me many things. Come and join with me.

A Cup of Tea

Sara and Zara sit on the chairs. They are gossiping. What a beautiful time!

They never think like this way.

Really good!
You are a magician.
How can you do this?

This is amazingly good.

Anyone here?
Customer calls.
Oh yeah!
We are open.
Pls take your seat and kindly let me know, how can I help you?

You, the waiter?
No.
I am the owner of this shop. Don't worry.
Say me anything you want.

That's impressive. Give me a lemon tea and a spicy masala tea...

Sure!
Give me 10 minutes only.

After some moments, oh hello sir!
You can take this book as your leisure company.
Oh sure!
What's that?
It's a poetry book. I am trying to write.

You are free to read and make any comment about this.

The book is ***You will be the winner***

That customer is reading the book.
In the meantime, the tea is ready.
He takes the cup and is trying to drink.
Wow!

It's really good. And your write is also good.
I like this.

Oh really!
Thank you so much.
If you want to say anyone about my book, then most welcome. And as for buying, you can get your copy from this tea corner, with a discount of 20 percent.

Oh so nice!
I will say my friends about your book.
I will take 2 copies.

Oh!
Thanks a lot for your words.
Here are your copies.
And pray for me.
I will be here all the time.

Hues!
Hues come from every corner of the tea shop. That is outstanding. Nobody can imagine what is inside. But the fact is, here is the soothing plot. Anyone can get the most important thing- tea, with the

most wonderful plot- poetry book. If wants, can take with his or herself, with a reasonable price.

It's the Hues of the dreamy lane.
Red, green, blue, purple, pink...there are lots of vibrant colours.
The Hues of heart!
Let's enjoy this time with the hues of the dearest life.

Copyright ©S Afrose, 20th Oct-24

Paint your pain!

Pain comes to drain your lane of dreams. How can you accept this time? The lane of the life-

Paint your pain with the beautiful crane.

A siren.

Wake up

Wake up!

It's time to walk and run.

What?
Can't?
Why?

Down it!

Don't say like this one. You will be the winner at last.

Be its owner

Be its ride.

Your pride-

You will make your crown...your expectation is flying up.

What a surprise!

Is that really occupied?

Of course dear. Just, paint your pain.

You will make tour of life, your footprints in this way of the paradise.

Copyright ©S Afrose, 21st Oct-24

Only for you!

I know

I miss you. Because you are no more here with me.

My love!

I love you so much.

Only for you, I can feel my heart. Now how can I survive?

I can't control myself.

Still, I can get that smell of the tea, you made. That was only for me.

I can't forget that moment.

That was very precious for me.

I am trying to get you into that cup of tea.

Only for you, as my mind seeks that fragrance of your heart.

This is love. My love!

Only for you, I am holding that cup of tea for a long time.

I want to stuck there forever.

Only for my love.

Copyright ©S Afrose, 21st Oct-24

Thank you so much
For being my friend
As usual,
Just love and love.
This is your favourite canvas.

Be happy.

From author and editorial desk of Bangladesh.

© S AFROSE, BD.

About the Author

S Afrose

"Author S Afrose (Sabiha Afrose from Bangladesh) has made her realm since August-2020. Her writes have been publishing on magazines and anthologies (90+). In this writing realm, she has achieved many awards (eg. Doctorate in Literature from Instituto Cultural Colombiano, Literoma Laureate Winner 2022, Mahatma Gandhi Award 2023 from Instituto Cultural Colombiano etc.

****
****

Published 31+ poetry books- Thanks Dear God, Poetic Essence , Reflection of Mind , Glittering Hopes, Angels Smile, Tiny Garden of Words, Dancing Alphabet, Artistic Muse, Essence of love, The Magical Quill, Dear Children, Haunted Site. Woman, The Butterfly, A Little Fantasy, Lion's Roar, The Bride, No War, Lost Lotus, Friendship, Happy Christmas, A New Beginning, Bluish Ocean, A Bouquet of Love, Stop Discrimination, Mirror, The Mask, Golden Wings of Time, Dear Mother, Race, Esshe Dana, Who I am?

****
****

All books are available on Amazon worldwide and also other sites as usual. She has written some bangla poetry books also. Her each write tries to reflect the core of the reality, as a decorated poetic flower.

Her new venture is working as a part of editorial team(Co-editor).

!st successful projrct is : VIBRANT THOUGHTS ,,,this poetry book is available for all, at all sites.

****

Educational achievements- B Pharm, M Pharm (JU,BD.)

Contact-

sabihapoetryparadise24@gmail.com

sabiha_pharma@yahoo.com

afrosewritings@outlook.com

YouTube: S Afrose *Muse of Writes*(@safrose_poetic_arts)

FacebookPage: Muse of Words by S Afrose

Twitter: @afrose2020

Instagram: @safrosepoetryworld

JUST A SIP,,,
WOULD YOU LIKE TO TAKE
"A CUP OF TEA"?

THANK YOU SO MUCH!

Milton Keynes UK
Ingram Content Group UK Ltd.
UKHW031342011224
451755UK00001B/193